First published in the US in 1936 by The Viking Press
First published in the UK in 2017
by Faber and Faber Ltd,
Bloomsbury House,
74–77 Great Russell Street, London WC1B 3DA
Printed in Europe

A CIP record for this book is available
from the British Library

ISBN 978–0–571–33596–1

4 6 8 10 9 7 5 3

A FABER HERITAGE PICTURE BOOK

The Story of
FERDINAND

By Munro Leaf

Illustrated by Robert Lawson

ff

Once upon a time in Spain

there was a little bull and
his name was Ferdinand.

All the other little bulls
he lived with would run
and jump and butt their
heads together,

but not Ferdinand.
He liked to sit just quietly
and smell the flowers.

He had a favourite spot out in the
pasture under a cork tree.

It was his favourite tree and he would sit
in its shade all day and smell the flowers.

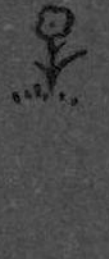

Sometimes his mother, who was a cow, would worry about him. She was afraid he would be lonesome all by himself.

'Why don't you run and play with the other little bulls and skip and butt your head?' she would say.

But Ferdinand would shake
his head. 'I like it better here
where I can sit just quietly
and smell the flowers.'

His mother saw that he was not lonesome,
and because she was an understanding mother,

even though she was a cow, she let him just
sit there and be happy.

As the years went by Ferdinand grew and grew until he was very big and strong. All the other bulls who had grown up with him in the same pasture would fight each other all day.

They would butt each other and stick each other with their horns. What they wanted most of all was to be picked to fight at the bull fights in Madrid.

But not Ferdinand –
he still liked to sit just quietly
under the cork tree
and smell the flowers.

One day five men came in
very funny hats to pick
the biggest,
fastest, roughest
bull to fight
in the
bull fights
in Madrid.

All the other bulls ran around
snorting and butting,
leaping and jumping
so the men
would think
they were
very,
very
strong and
fierce and
pick them.

Ferdinand knew that they wouldn't pick him and he didn't care. So he went out to his favourite cork tree to sit down.

He didn't look where he was sitting and
instead of sitting on the nice cool grass
in the shade he sat on a bumble bee.

Well, if you were a bumble bee
and a bull sat on you what would
you do? You would sting him.
And that is just what this bee did
to Ferdinand.

Wow! Did it hurt!

Ferdinand jumped up with a snort. He ran around puffing and snorting, butting and pawing the ground as if he were crazy.

The five men saw him and
they all shouted with joy. Here
was the largest and fiercest bull of
all. Just the one for the bull fights
in Madrid!

So they took him away
for the bull fight day
in a cart.

What a day it was!
Flags were flying,
bands were playing . . .

and all the lovely ladies had
flowers in their hair.

They had a parade into the bull ring.

First came the Banderilleros
with long sharp pins with ribbons on them
to stick in the bull and make him angry.

Next came the Picadores who rode skinny horses and they had long spears to stick in the bull and make him even more angry.

Then came the Matador,
the proudest of all –
he thought he was very
handsome, and bowed
to the ladies.
He had a
red cape and a sword
and was supposed to
stick the bull last of all.

Then came the bull, and you know
who that was, don't you?
– FERDINAND.

They called him Ferdinand the Fierce
and all the Banderilleros were afraid
of him and the Picadores
were afraid of him and the
Matador was
scared stiff.

Ferdinand ran to
the middle of
the ring and
everyone shouted
and clapped
because they
thought he
was going to
fight fiercely
and butt and
snort and stick
his horns around.

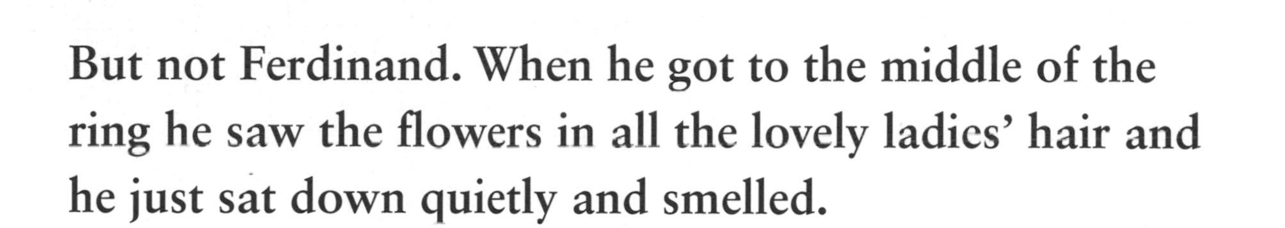

But not Ferdinand. When he got to the middle of the ring he saw the flowers in all the lovely ladies' hair and he just sat down quietly and smelled.

He wouldn't fight and be fierce no matter what they did. He just sat and smelled. And the Banderilleros were angry and the Picadores were even more angry and the Matador was so angry he cried because he couldn't show off with his cape and sword.

So they had to take
Ferdinand home.

And for all I know he is sitting there still,
under his favourite cork tree, smelling the flowers
just quietly.

He is very happy.

THE END

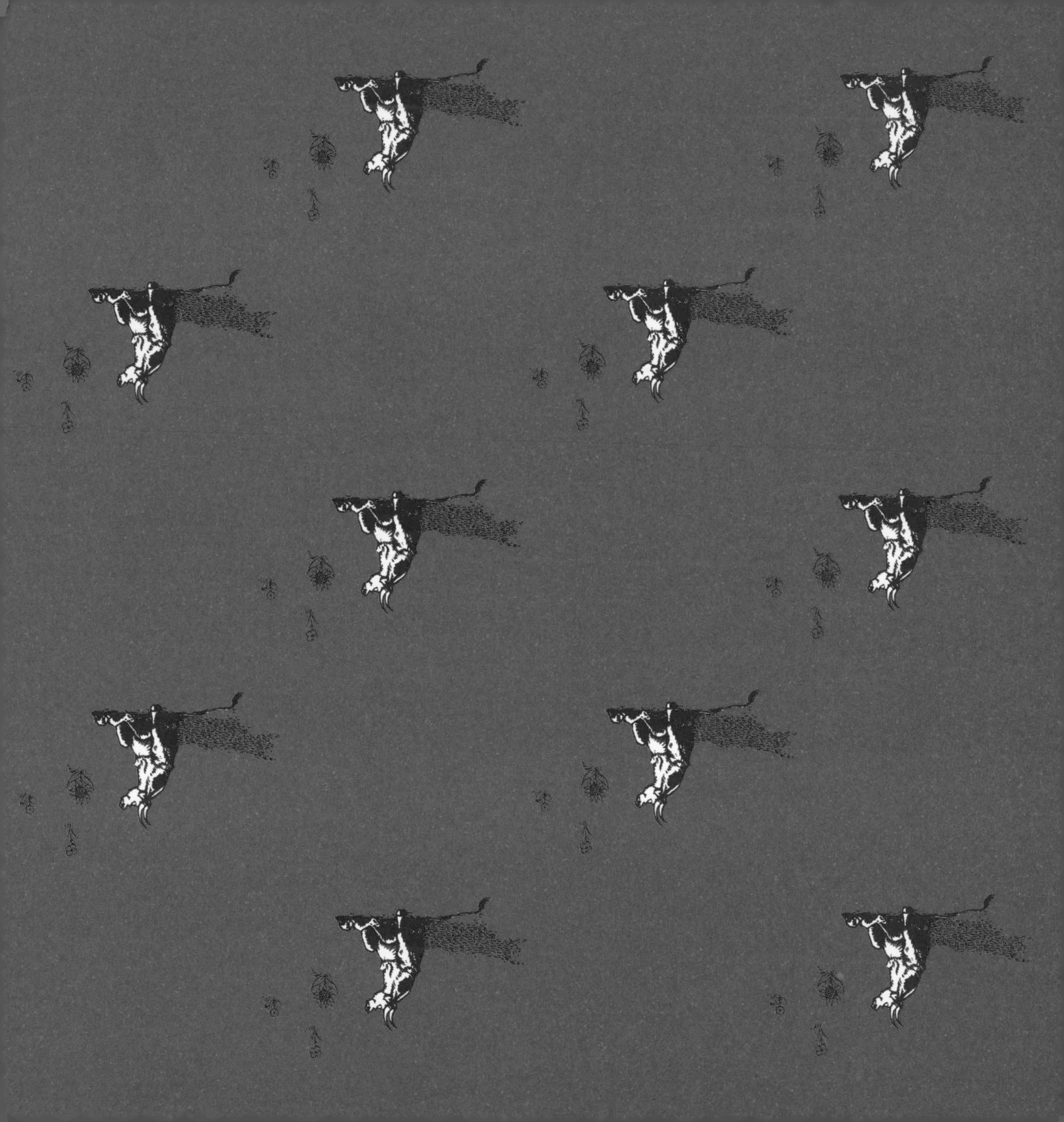

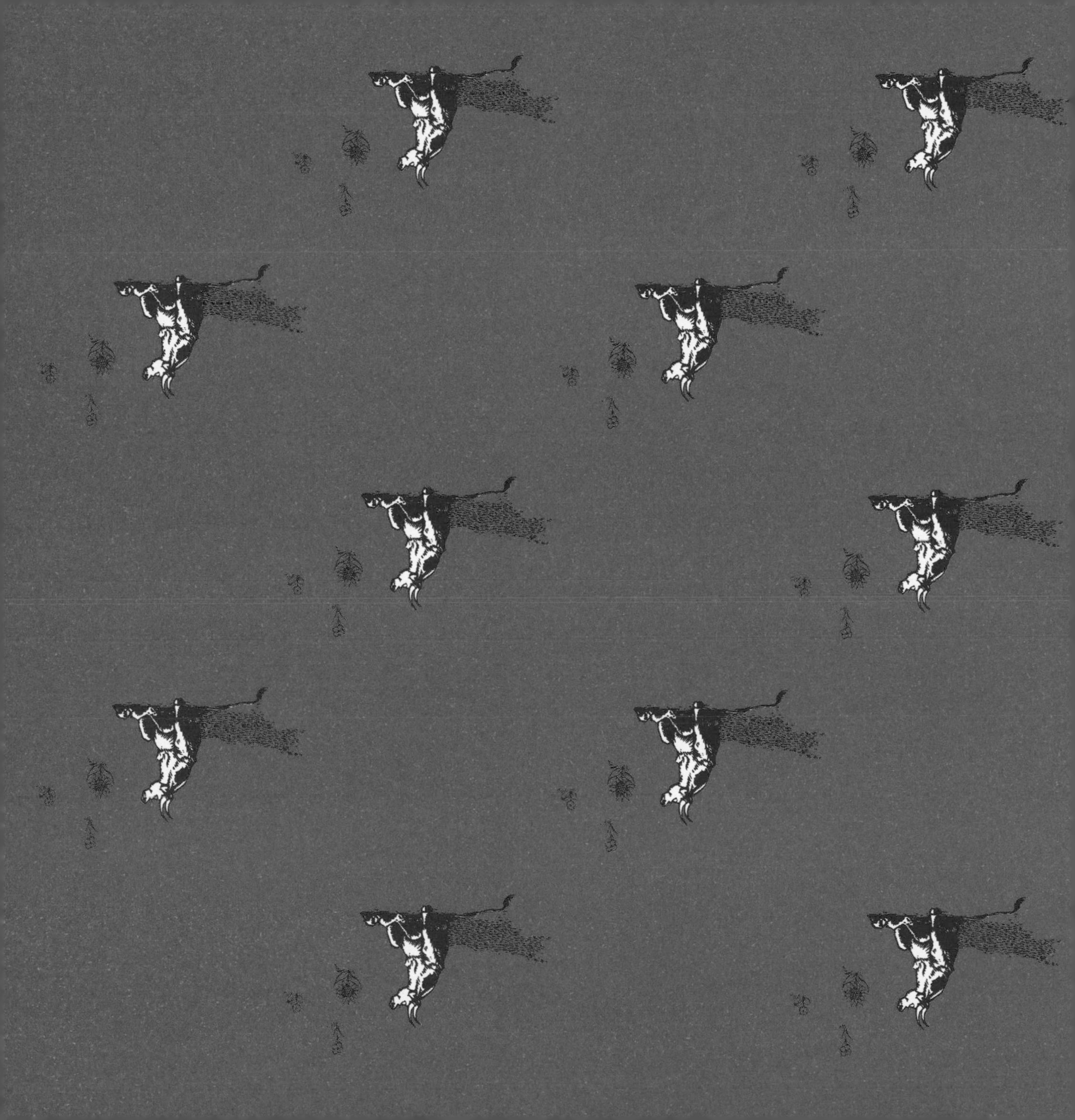

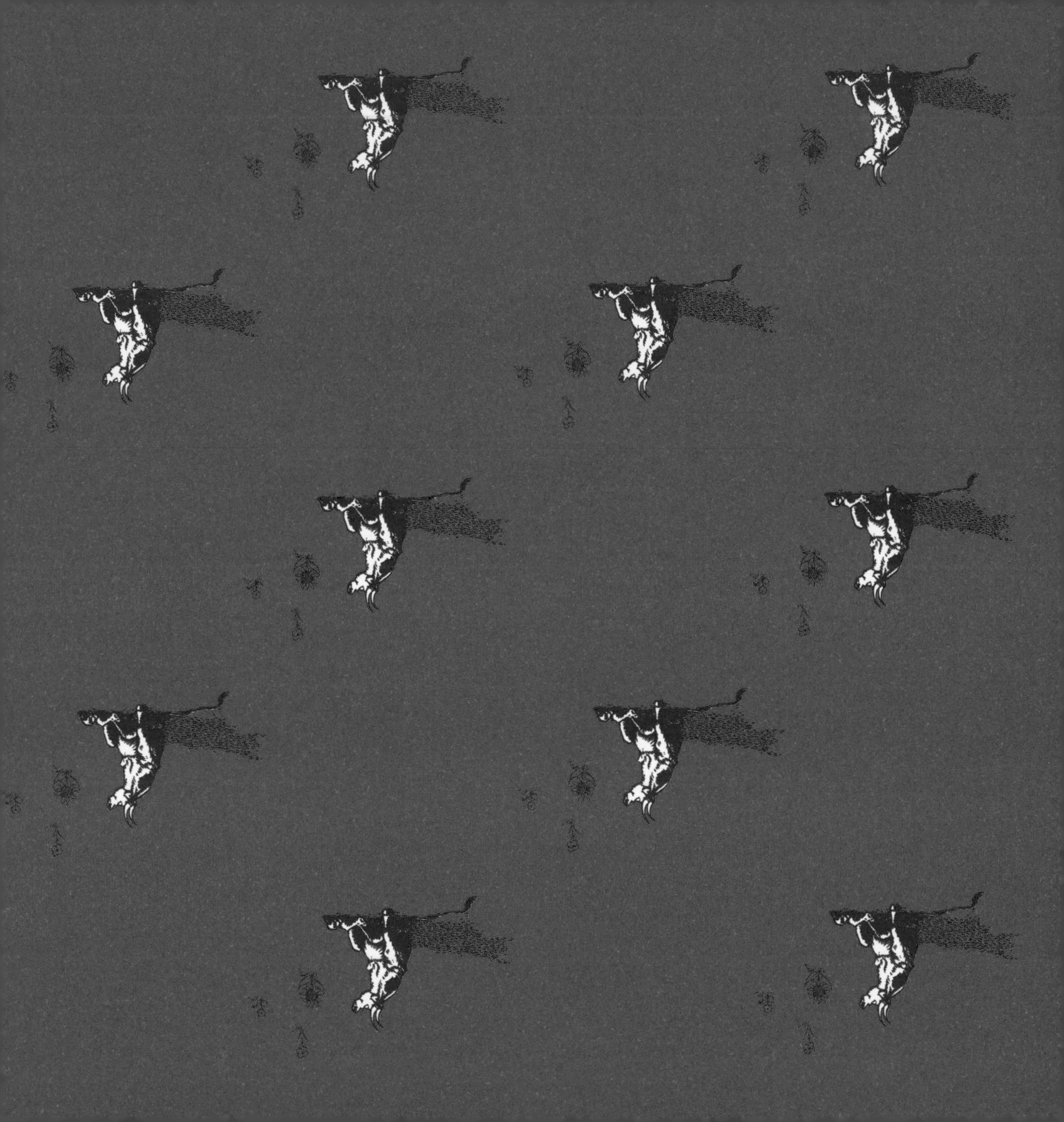